GREEN VS. MEAN

By Geof Smith
Illustrated by Steve Lambe

A GOLDEN BOOK • NEW YORK

Published in the United States by Golden Books, an imprint of Random House Children's Books, a division of Random House, Inc., 1745 Broadway, New York, NY 10019, and in Canada by Random House of Canada Limited, Toronto.

Based on characters created by Peter Laird and Kevin Eastman.
ISBN 978-0-449-81765-0
randomhouse.com/kids
Printed in the United States of America
10 9 8 7 6 5 4 3 2 1

Many years ago, a strange chemical turned four regular turtles into powerful mutants. Now they live in a secret hideaway deep beneath the streets of New York City.

They're strong.

They're brothers.

They're always ready for adventure.

They're the Teenage Mutant Ninja Turtles!

Leonardo is the leader. He's serious, and he's dedicated to his martial arts studies.

Donatello is a brilliant inventor. He can build anything from parts he finds in the sewers.

Raphael is the toughest Turtle. He's lean, green, and ready for battle.

Michelangelo is the youngest. He's always ready to pull a prank or tell a joke.

The Turtles' underground lair is an awesome hangout where they watch television, play video games, and even skateboard.

PIZZA
PIZZA
PIZZA
PIZZA

Splinter was once a man, but he mutated . . . into a giant rat. Now he teaches the Turtles the ways of the ninja. The Turtles train hard and learn about offensive attacks, defensive poses, and sneaking through the shadows.

But mainly they learn that it's really hard to be a ninja.

Sometimes the Turtles sneak out of their secret lair at night and visit the streets of New York.

"Remember, guys, we can't be seen," Leonardo says. "Four giant turtles might freak people out."

The city is busy and exciting. It's filled with action, adventure, and best of all . . . PIZZA!

But the Turtles must be careful, because the city is also full of fearsome foes.

The Kraang are invaders from another dimension who want to take over the planet Earth. They are fleshy pink aliens that live inside robots called Kraang-droids. The Kraang-droids can disguise themselves to look just like humans! They made the strange chemical that mutated Splinter and the Turtles.

Shredder, the most powerful martial arts master in the world, commands a fierce army of ninjas called the Foot Clan. He is an old enemy of the Turtles' teacher, Splinter. Shredder has vowed to destroy Splinter and the Turtles.

Xever was a master criminal until he was exposed to the mutagen made by the Kraang. Now he is Fishface, a giant fishlike creature with a poisonous bite. A scientist built him robot legs, so he can run on land.

While searching for the Turtles, ninja master Chris Bradford was also splashed with mutagen. He became a powerful half-man, half-dog creature called Dogpound. He's fiercely loyal to his martial arts master, Shredder.

The Turtles are not alone in their battles against the bad guys. A teenage girl named April O'Neil helps them. April's father is a great scientist who has been captured by the Kraang, and she is on a mission to find him.

Wherever there is evil, Leonardo, Donatello, Raphael, and Michelangelo will be there to stop it.

"Time to bash some bots!" yells Raphael.

After their battles, the Turtles return to the safety of their lair to celebrate.

"Ahh," sighs Michelangelo. "Victory tastes like pizza."

PIZZA
PIZZA
PIZZA
PIZZA
PIZZA

Turtle power!